This book is dedicated to the
staff, interns and volunteers of
Clearwater Marine Aquarium's
Sea Turtle Nesting Team.

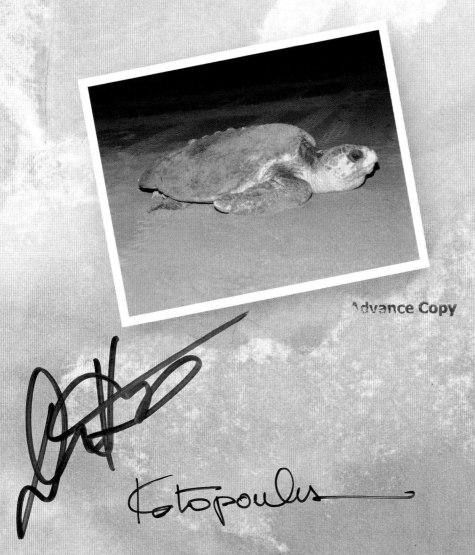

Advance Copy

Kotopoulis

Acknowledgments

Thanks to everyone who believed in this project and helped make it a reality including:

David Yates, Janice Wood, Maddie Hightower, Tyler Rowland,
Tracy Philbeck, and Beth Friederich.

The author wishes to give a special thanks to Kotopoulis who donated his
incredible sense of humor and artistic talent.

This book is dedicated to the staff, interns and volunteers of
Clearwater Marine Aquarium's Sea Turtle Nesting Team.

Clearwater, Florida

Published by Clearwater Marine Aquarium

Design and Layout
Tyler Rowland and Tracy Philbeck

Photo Credits: © Clearwater Marine Aquarium

ISBN 978-0-9908229-0-5

First Edition, February 2015

Captain Tortuga

and the

Treasure of Sand Key

Written by David Kinne

Illustrated by Kotopoulis

Published by Clearwater Marine Aquarium

I be Captain Tortuga,
the fiercest treasure hunter
in these here seven seas,
and this be my trusty bird, Polly.
Say Hello Polly. POLLY?
She's quiet for a parrot.
This here be my story about the time I found
the most valuable treasure of all:

The Treasure of
Sand Key!

It all started when my ship, the Caretta Clipper,
was anchored off the coast of Clearwater, Florida
near a small island called Sand Key.
I had taken Polly ashore for a much needed vacation
when I came across some people from
Clearwater Marine Aquarium.

I casually crept closer, listening
to their conversation.
They didn't notice me, of course,
because I blend like a pirate ninja!

As they were talking,
my eyes lit up.
They were talking about
a buried treasure!
It was hard to hear,
but from what I gathered,
the only one who knew exactly
where this treasure was buried
was a beautiful sea turtle named

Lilly the Loggerhead.

You see, Lilly was hit
by a speeding motor boat
and was rescued by
Clearwater Marine Aquarium.
They were able to nurse her back to health.
and release her back to the sea.
And she had this treasure map locked away
in her loggerhead noggin!

When she was hit by the boat,
Lilly got an unusual mark on her shell.

This was how
I would identify her.

My plan was simple.
I had to find Lilly
and follow her to the treasure!

Ah treasure! Gold, jewels.
I could almost taste them,
right Polly? POLLY?
This bird never talks.
For months I scoured the Seven Seas
in search of this special turtle.

After hundreds of dives,
I finally found her off the coast of Brazil!
Sea turtles travel thousands of miles
to their feeding grounds.
I set sail after her.
The treasure was within my grasp!

As we traveled north,
Lilly got caught in the net
of a commercial shrimp boat.
I thought this might be
the end of Lilly and of my hopes
for finding this treasure.
Casting fear aside,
I dove into the water after her,
cutlass in me mouth planning to
release her from the perilous netting.

Luckily, the large net had
a Turtle Excluder Device or T.E.D.
The bars of this contraption
kept Lilly from being captured by the net
and she was able to swim free.

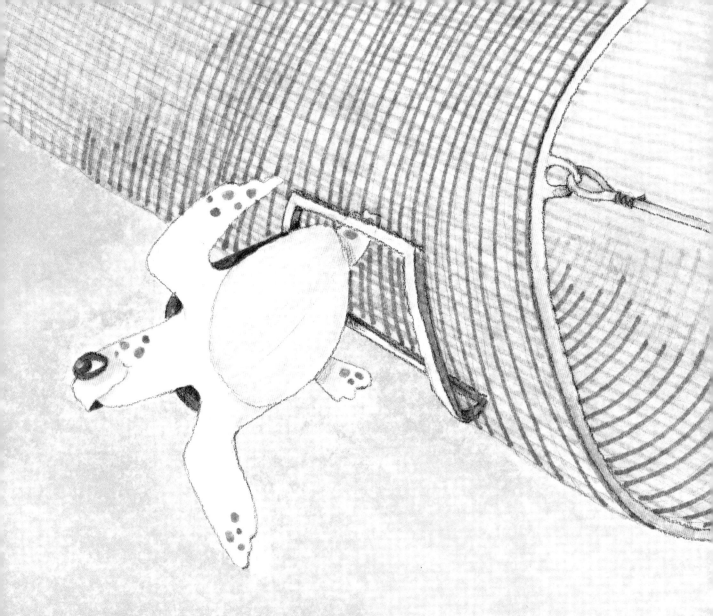

That was a close call indeed!
But Lilly swam off northward
toward the treasure.

Off the coast of the Bahamas,
I noticed Lilly feeding on jellyfish.
They don't look all that tasty to me or Polly, but
these turtles love them.
Then I noticed Lilly making a mad dash
for a very strange jellyfish.
Just as she was about to take a bite,
I plunged into the sea
and grabbed it away from her.
It wasn't a jellyfish at all. It was a plastic bag that
someone had carelessly thrown away.
But it looked just like a jellyfish to Lilly.

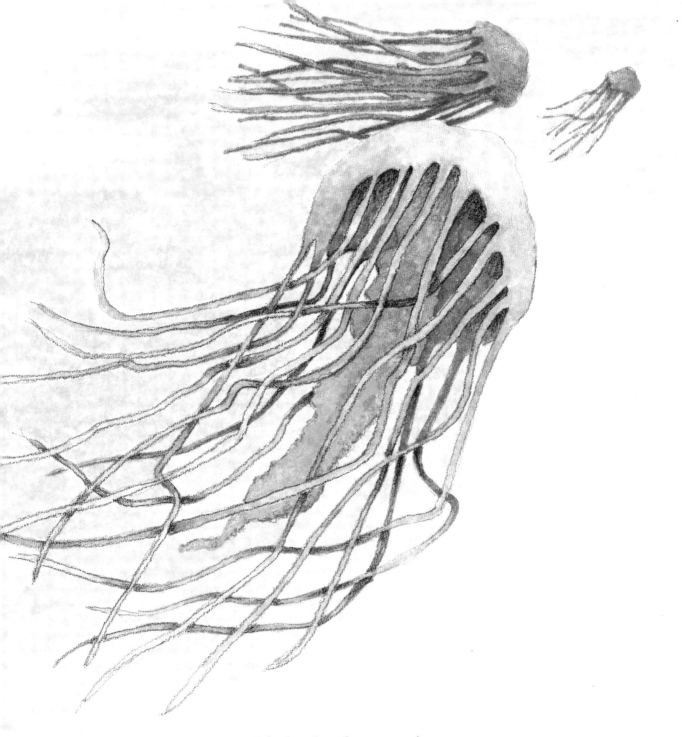

If she had eaten it,
she surely could have choked.
Another close call!
But Lilly was safe and on her way.
And I followed to the treasure!

It wasn't long before I realized
we were entering the warm waters
of the Gulf of Mexico.
The shallow coastline was peppered with
pleasure boats and people fishing.
As Lilly traveled through these waters,

her flippers became entangled in
some discarded fishing line.
Another serious hazard!
Again I dove into the sea,
and managed to free Lilly
from the dangerous situation.
Keeping Lilly safe was becoming
a full time job!
But it was all worth it as long as I could find me treasure.

Finally we approached our destination.
And lo and behold it was the very same beach
where people from the aquarium released Lilly
on Sand Key!
Under the cover of darkness,
the turtle crawled up onto the beach.
Then she turned around and
began making her way back
to the sea.

She wasn't digging for the treasure!
I noticed some folks from
Clearwater Marine Aquarium on the beach
and asked them why.
They called it a "false crawl."
It was the lights, they explained.
The lights were too bright
and confused poor Lilly.

I offered to use my cannons
from the Caretta Clipper
to blast the infernal lights to smithereens,
but they suggested we just
talk to the people instead.

I supposed we could try it their way,
but kept me cannons at the ready.

Just in case.

Quickly, we all ran to the
nearby homes and businesses
and asked them to turn out their lights.

The beach darkened and Lilly turned around
back toward the shore.
Finally, she found the special spot
and began to dig in the moist sand
with her back flippers.
Visions of jewels and gold doubloons
danced in my head as I waited for my treasure.

Then she stopped digging.
She began laying eggs!

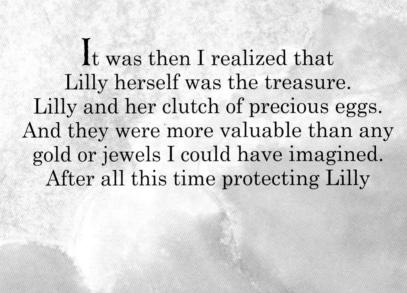

It was then I realized that
Lilly herself was the treasure.
Lilly and her clutch of precious eggs.
And they were more valuable than any
gold or jewels I could have imagined.
After all this time protecting Lilly

from the many hazards in the ocean,
I knew I had found a new purpose.
That's when I decided to volunteer
at Clearwater Marine Aquarium
and join my new friends
on the Sea Turtle Nesting Team!

After my friend, Lilly, laid her eggs,
she returned to the gulf
and swam off toward her feeding grounds.

But my work was just beginning.
I had to keep this treasure safe!

My new friends from
the Sea Turtle Nesting Team
gave me four stakes to put into the sand
and some ribbon to mark the new nest.
Then they placed a plastic cage over the nest

to keep away pesky predators like birds
who might want to eat the eggs.

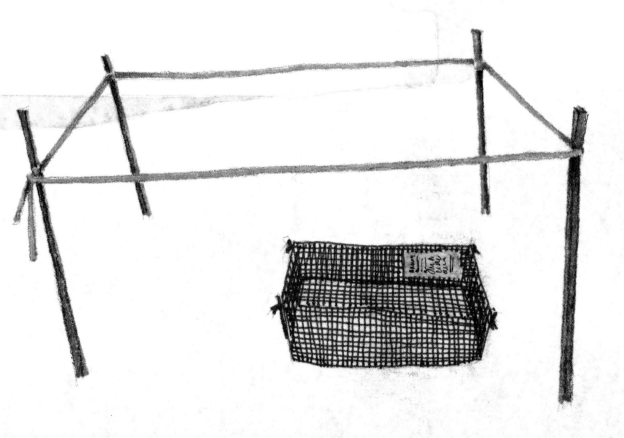

So here I stand,
on guard on this balmy summer night.
Captain Tortuga and his trusty friend Polly,
protecting the real treasure of Sand Key,
until the eggs hatch and hundreds of
wee Lilly and Leroy Loggerheads
make their way to freedom
and safety of the briny depths.

Did You Know?

There are only seven species of sea turtles in the world and all of them are endangered! Mother sea turtles come back to lay their eggs on the exact same beach where they were born. Sea turtles spend their entire lives swimming in the ocean. The only exception is when the females come on to land to build their nests and lay their eggs. The largest species of sea turtle is the leatherback. It can grow to nearly 2000 lbs and eats its weight in jellyfish every day! The temperature of a sea turtle's nest determines whether the hatchlings will be boys or girls. When the sand is warmer, more females will be born. Cooler sand produces more males.

A fun way to remember this is "Hot Chicks, Cool Dudes".

How Can You Help?

Become a Sea Turtle Guardian!
Head over to **www.seewinter.com/turtleguardians** and register.
You will receive a monthly newsletter chock full of information, pictures and videos all about the Sea Turtle Program at Clearwater Marine Aquarium.

About Clearwater Marine Aquarium and Sea Turtle Nesting
A 501(c)(3) non-profit organization, Clearwater Marine Aquarium's mission is to preserve marine life and the environment while inspiring the human spirit through leadership in education, research, rescue, rehabilitation and release. In addition to sea turtle rehabilitation work, Clearwater Marine Aquarium staff and volunteers monitor nearly 26 miles of Pinellas County's coast line and report on any nesting activity. The combination of releasing injured and sick turtles back into the wild while ensuring as many hatchlings as possible make it into the Gulf is our way of protecting these species from extinction.